WEEKEND RETREAT

Brenda Hyslip

WEEKEND RETREAT

TATE PUBLISHING & *Enterprises*

Weekend Retreat
Copyright © 2010 by Brenda Hyslip. All rights reserved.

No part of this publication may be reproduced, stored in a retrieval system or transmitted in any way by any means, electronic, mechanical, photocopy, recording or otherwise without the prior permission of the author except as provided by USA copyright law.

This novel is a work of fiction. Names, descriptions, entities, and incidents included in the story are products of the author's imagination. Any resemblance to actual persons, events, and entities is entirely coincidental.

The opinions expressed by the author are not necessarily those of Tate Publishing, LLC.

Published by Tate Publishing & Enterprises, LLC
127 E. Trade Center Terrace | Mustang, Oklahoma 73064 USA
1.888.361.9473 | www.tatepublishing.com

Tate Publishing is committed to excellence in the publishing industry. The company reflects the philosophy established by the founders, based on Psalm 68:11, *"The Lord gave the word and great was the company of those who published it."*

Book design copyright © 2010 by Tate Publishing, LLC. All rights reserved.
Cover design by Brandon Wood
Interior design by Jeff Fisher

Published in the United States of America

ISBN: 978-1-61663-086-7
1. Fiction, Thrillers
2. Fiction, Mystery & Detective, General
10.04.06

Dedication

To all the parents who take the time to hear what their children are telling them. We were given two ears and one mouth for one reason: to listen twice as much as we talk.

Past, present, and future.

Weekend Retreat

Maya watched Zack, her little brother, as he stepped of the airplane. He looked good very good, she thought, in his jeans and blazer. How long had it been she tried to remember since they had seen each other? To long she thought and I am mostly to blame for that. She felt guilty and ashamed. I should have tried harder, she told herself especially since we were lucky enough to find each other again after all these years of separation.

"Hello Sis," Zack's deep voice brought Maya back to the present. She looked good, she looked healthy and he told her so. Flattery will get you a great dinner Maya could not help but smile she had prepared what used to be their favorite meal Mamas special lasagna. She knew that her little brother not really remembered it he had been to young but she remembered she had watched him eat it many times. But right now they needed to get his luggage and leave this crowded airport.

How will he react? She wondered what will his answer be when he finds out why I asked him to come! How much did they really know about each other's lives after all they had been separated so many years ago when she was a young girl and him still a baby. She had no idea but right now they needed each other. She needed him to go on a journey with her to face the past and find some answers a journey that Maya thought that they would never have to go on. Would he be willing to help? We will see, she told herself; I will find out in the next few days.

A while later, in the car, Zack asked Maya, "How are you really doing, sis, and how are the nightmares? Are you still having them?"

For a moment, Maya got very quiet, but then she turned her head to look at Zack, and with a low voice she told her brother. "Let's go to the house so we can eat and then over a good glass of wine we will talk. You are a grown man now, twenty-two years old, and it is time for me to tell you as best as I can remember what actually happened to the three of us all those years ago."

Deal Zack smiled, and then brother and sister retreated into their own thoughts for the rest of the drive. Finally, they arrived at Maya's house.

"So this is it, all these beautiful flowers." Maya could tell that Zack loved her little place.

"Maybe you will stay here for a very long time," she told him. "Maybe forever you could work here. I hear that you are a very good private investigator; you would find plenty of work here."

"That same goes for you, sis. You are a very good nurse; you could come to New York and have plenty of work there."

True, now they both laughed as they walked into the house.

"Oh, I can smell the lasagna." Zack rolled his eyes. "Being a confirmed bachelor, I don't get a home-cooked meal very often."

"Well, everything is ready; let's eat," Maya said, and so they did. After the meal, they cleaned the kitchen together, and when that was done, they took a bottle of wine, two glasses, and went outside to sit on the patio.

It was a beautiful summer evening, and after a few minutes of silence, Maya began her story.

※

"You know that our parents were very, very rich. Papa owned a paper factory, and we lived in a beautiful house with many servants. You were only two years old when it all began. I was six years old, and your brother, Bryan, was eight. Our parents had many friends and partied often. They also took many, many trips, and some of them were two months long. There was this place called Weekend Retreat where we had to stay when they traveled. It was a beautiful retreat, very expensive, so only the rich could afford to leave their children there…"

The first time they took us was just for three or four days. Our rooms were beautiful, and I know Mama and Papa thought that their children were in the best of care. We went to the dining room, had dinner, and then we were each given a small glass of juice. That was on a Thursday. The next thing I remember was someone telling me to get up, take a shower, and go to the dining room where our parents were waiting. We had a great lunch, and then we got into the car that would take us home. Bryan did not say much; I did not say much; you were the only one jabbering away.

"'Well, what did you do all weekend long?' we heard papa's voice. 'Did you have lots of fun? Did you make new friends?' Bryan looked at me. 'It was fine,' I heard him answer. Leave the children alone, Mama interrupted. They look well rested; they must have had a wonderful time.

Later that evening, Bryan took my arm. Maya I don't remember anything. What did we do for the last three days?

I don't know Bryan, I told him. I don't remember anything either. I can't explain it. Let's hope we will never have to see that place again; it gives me the creeps. But that was not to be. Three weeks later, our parents informed us that they were going on another four-day trip, and that we had to go back to Weekend Retreat. Why can't we stay home? We pleaded with our mother. 'We would not be alone;

we have Alice, our maid, here; we would be fine. Please, Mama, let us stay home.'

'What are you asking me? Mama was appalled. I will not leave my children with the hired help and what about your little brother? No, you are staying in the nicest place in the whole country. We will not have to worry knowing that you are at the retreat.' And that was when I knew arguing would not help, so we went again. We ate dinner, and the next thing we remembered was that we showered, had lunch, and went back home. Bryan and I became very, very close during that time. We only talked to each other. Our parents were so busy with their own lives; they did not seem to notice. This went on for about two more years. Then one day they informed us that they were going on a three-month European trip and that the three of us would have to stay at Weekend Retreat. Bryan and I panicked; we considered running away, but we had no money, so we knew that we would not get very far.

Bryan hugged me and said, "we will watch out for each other." Maybe the three months will go by fast, and then when we are back home we will make our parents listen to us. I am ten now, and you are almost eight; they will have to listen to us.

I felt a little better. At least we had each other, and three months was really not that long. And so it was. The next two weeks were very, very busy—lots of shopping for new clothes. After all, we would grow in three months, and Mama wanted us to have everything that she thought we would need, and before we knew it we were back at the retreat. After a tearful goodbye, we were ushered into the dining room had a wonderful dinner and were handed our glass of juice."

※

Maya looked up at Zack. His face was like a white mask. She got worried. Are you all right? Little brother, do you want me to stop?

He shook his head no. "Maya, don't stop. I had no idea about any of this."

"But how could you have, Zack? You were only a little boy." And with that, she continued.

※

"I only saw Bryan one more time after we arrived. I remember eating every few days, and the rest is a blank. About two and a half months into the stay, Bryan and I were called in to an office where we saw an older man sitting behind a large desk. You were not there. 'Where is Zack? Where is our little brother? We both asked at the same time.

"'Slow down,' the man in the white coat told us. 'I will answer all of your questions, but first I have some sad news for you. There has been a boating accident, on one of their outings and your parents did not survive.

"'You mean they are dead?' we asked. It did not sink in what the man was telling us.

"'I am sorry,' he said again. He did not look sorry.

"'What about Zack, our little brother?' I heard Bryan's voice.

"'Your father's brother picked him up. He and his wife will take him in, but they are not willing to take the three of you. But I have some good news. Your parents made us temporary guardians over everything that they own, including your trust funds while they were gone, so you can stay here until you become of age. From now on you need to look at Weekend Retreat as your new home. Of course, you will live in a different section of the Retreat and you will be given some chores to earn your stay.'

"'We don't want to live here,' Bryan and I said stubbornly, but the man just smiled and told us, 'You have no choice. As I said before you are not of legal age, so I suggest that you make the best of this situation.' And with those words we were dismissed.

"Outside his door stood a man and a woman who waited to take us both to our new living quarters. That was the last time that I saw our brother."

"The new room was tiny; there was one small metal bed and one small dresser. The bathroom was down the hall for everybody to use. I was horrified. Did people really live like this?

"'Where are my things?' I asked the woman.

"You will not need them anymore,' she told me. "I will get you a uniform that you will wear. You are one of us now, so the sooner that you get used to your new life, the better it will be for you." And with that, she left. I sat down on the bed. I felt nothing. I needed to cry. I thought, *why can't I cry?* But the tears just would not come.

"Shortly after, I was handed my uniform and shoes. Again, I was horrified, but I put them on. I looked into the mirror. Was I looking at the same girl that I saw yesterday? I didn't think so; I hardly recognized myself.

The uniform consisted of a pair of grey pants and a grey top. Both were at least two sizes to big

I had never seen anything so ugly. What was it made out of? It felt like sandpaper on my skin.

"'This is just a terrible nightmare,' I told myself. 'I will wake up soon, and our parents will be here to pick us up.' But that was not to be. The lady came back and said, in a sharp tone 'Let's go now; it is time for you to start working.'

"And we worked and worked from early morning until late into the night .We cleaned, we washed, and we cleaned some more. Twice a day, we were allowed to eat—and that was not very much. When new children arrived, we sometimes could have some of their leftovers and the same after they had left with their parents. This went on for about three years. Every time I asked about Bryan, I was told that he was no longer my concern and that he was fine. Then, one day I was ordered to help out in a different section of the retreat. I followed the woman who looked like a nurse without saying a word I had learned by now not to ask questions. What I saw next chilled me to the bones. What was this a Hospital? It could not be a hospital it was a retreat, but there were all these stretchers with sleeping children. There must have been close to a hundred of them. I stared in disbelief.

"The nurse handed me a list with nothing but numbers on it and told me, the children on the cots with these numbers are leaving today. You need to check every cot and make sure that the number matches the number on your sheet. If it does, pull the bed to the left side of the room.

"I did what I was told, and an hour later, all the cots with the matching numbers were on the left side of the room.

"'Good job,' she told me. 'Now we will wake them up, and you will help me get them showered and dressed.' And with that she pulled a medicine cart close to the first cot. I could not say a word; I just watched in horror as she took a needle and syringe and gave everyone an injection. She looked at me once, smiled, and told me, 'You are doing fine; you will get used to this in no time. I think I like you.' She went on. 'I am going to see if I can get them to let you come to this section to work with me. The work is not as hard over here; it would make your life a little easier' and with that she continued with the shots.

"A few minutes later, the children started to wake up. The girls were ushered in to the biggest shower that I had ever seen, and the boys into theirs on the other side. And after they had been cleaned and dressed, they went to the dining room to be greeted by their parents and to have lunch with them.

"That evening in my room, my mind was racing. *What was going on here? Is that why we could never remember anything when we had to stay here?* These monsters were putting these children into an induced coma. 'Oh, please, God,' I prayed. 'Help me to get to work over there. I need to find out if that's what had happened to Bryan, Zack, and me.' And my prayers were answered. Two days later, I was moved to the other building. By now I was fourteen.

"'By the way, my name is Phyllis,' the nurse who had helped me to come to this building told me one day. 'I am sure we will make a good team.

If you do what I tell you to do and if you don't talk to anybody about our work here, your life will be a lot better than it was before.'

"And so we worked. Each time new children arrived, they were put to sleep after their last meal with their parents. We woke them up every four days to get them cleaned and ready to go to the dining room to eat. Then the juice that they were given after the meal would put them back into a deep sleep for the next four days. Sometimes at night in my bed I thought, *what is wrong with these parents? Why don't they wonder why their children had no stories to tell about what they had done here?* Were they really so involved in their own lives or did they simply not care? They paid such enormous amounts of money for their children to stay here; I could not believe that nobody ever questioned anything. This place was worse than a hellhole.

So the Years Went By

One day, I told Phyllis that I had a brother here too. 'Bryan is eighteen now. He must be waiting for me to turn eighteen so we can leave here together. We promised each other that one would not leave without the other. I have not seen or heard from him in all these years, but I am sure that he is here and waiting.' Phyllis listened to me carefully but did not say anything. 'Maybe you could find out, something' I kept on. 'I just want to know that he is all right.'

"'I will see what I can do,' she finally told me, and with that we went back to our duties.

"About a month after that, I started getting really good food and lots of fruit to eat. 'Why am I getting all that good stuff?' I asked Phyllis one day.

"She smiled. 'You are such a good worker, but you are a little thin for your age, so we decided to fatten you up a bit. Enjoy it. 'And I did. I really did. It brought back long-forgotten memories when we were home with our parents and we had all this good food. For the first time in years, I felt really healthy and strong. Only six more months and I would be eighteen, and Bryan and I could leave. We would have plenty of money. I knew our parents had left us a large trust fund. We would get our little brother Zack, and together we would start a new life. Oh, the future looked so bright."

Still dreaming the door to my room opened. What was happening and who were these two men? I had never seen them before. I suddenly felt fear I could not catch my breath. One man looked like a doctor and I noticed that he was holding a syringe in his hand I was not sick I was feeling good, better than I had felt in years. I looked at Phyllis who had come to see me earlier but Phyllis did not say a word. Now both men stood beside my bed. "Relax, I am a doctor. Give me your arm." The older man told me. No I told him as I tucked both of my arms under the blanket but before I could say anything else the other man an orderly pulled my arm out and the next thing that I remember was pain incredible pain. I tried to scream but the medicine worked fast not one sound came out of my mouth.

※

"I opened my eyes. I was in a room that looked like a hospital room. Both of my arms were connected to IV tubes. What was going on? I did not remember being sick. Then the door opened and a doctor walked toward my bed.

"'Good morning. How are you feeling?' Was that a smile? I could not be sure.

"'I am fine,' I told him. 'But please tell me what happened. I don't remember being sick and how long have I been here?'

"'Slow down.' He smiled. You had a ruptured appendix, and you have been here twenty days.'

"'Twenty days,' I cried. 'That's not possible.' But he put his hand on my arm and told me, 'Don't worry. We took the bad appendix out, and you will feel as good as new in just a few more weeks. Phyllis is watching over you like a mother over her child. In some people, the healing just takes a little bit longer.'

"'I will be as good as new?' I asked the doctor again.

"'Yes, you will,' he reassured me a second time. 'But now it is time for you to rest.' And the last thing that I saw was him injecting something into my IV.

"It took a few more weeks, but then I did start to feel better and pretty soon I went back to work. I asked Phyllis one more time about Bryan, but her answer was the same as before.

"'Honey, he left when he turned eighteen,' she said. I simply could not believe that. Something told me that he would not have left here without trying to contact me. But I kept that thought to myself, and after that, I did not ask about Bryan again.

"The next few months went by much to slow, but finally the long-awaited day arrived when I turned eighteen. I made an appointment to see the headmaster so I could tell him that I was leaving.

"'We are so very disappointed in you,' he told me. 'We were hoping that you would stay on at

Weekend Retreat. Besides, tell me what will you do on the outside?'

"'I have money,' I told him, lots of money. I will go back to school just as soon as I locate my two brothers.'

"'So you really think that you have money?' The man laughed out loud. Let me tell you 'You don't have a dime. Your parents gave us custody over you, your brothers and your money. Do you think that your room and board here all these years has been free?'

Our parents were rich I told him and I was old enough to know that my brothers and I had large trust funds what happened to that? . He studied her carefully could she possibly cause him any problems?

He quickly decided that she could not he had paid her father s brother the one who had taken Zack a large sum of money in exchange for custody of Bryan and her and he had also paid large amounts to people who had the power to legalize the rest of the papers. These kids had brought him millions and he had made sure that everything was legal. No he smiled to himself he had nothing to worry about.

"I started feeling sick. 'I worked from early morning until late into the night,' I stuttered, 'with very little to eat and only a uniform to my name. I should have gotten paid for all my work.'

"'Well, I can see how ungrateful you are.' His voice was like ice now. 'Go get your things and leave. I never want to see your face again.'

"I have no memory how I got back to my room, but when I walked in, the bed was already stripped, and my few belongings packed. Phyllis saw the panic in my eyes, and when she and I were alone for a few minutes, she handed me an envelope and whispered, hide this quickly. There are a few dollars for bus fare and an address to a shelter. I have a friend who runs the place. I will call her as soon as you are of these premises. I know she will try to help you.' She hugged me quickly. Did I see tears in her eyes, or did I imagine them? Later, I was not sure.

"Then an orderly came took me by the arm and said, 'Let's go, missy.' And a few minutes later, I was locked outside the main gate. I sat down on my little suitcase and cried and cried, and when there were no more tears, I opened the envelope that Phyllis had given me. I found a few dollars, directions to the bus station, and the address to the shelter. I started walking for how long I don't remember but finally I arrived at the bus station. I got on the bus so much had happened and I had no Idea what I was going to do and besides where was Bryan? But before I could think about anything else I arrived at the bus stop where I had to get off.

"The lady who greeted me at the door smiled. 'You must be Maya,' she said. 'I am Pam I am in charge of this shelter,' Phyllis called me and told me to look for you. Well, come in and have something to eat; you must be hungry. Then go upstairs and get a good night's sleep. Tomorrow we will talk and try to figure out what we can do.'"

Maya looked up at her little brother. He had not moved. His face was pain stricken, and tears were running down his cheeks.

"Oh, Maya," he said quietly. "I had no idea how you and Bryan must have suffered all those years. I asked my uncle once why you did not live with us, and he told me that you wanted to stay at the retreat and that you were happy there. I wish I had known."

"Oh, Zack Maya touched his face. "You were a little boy, barely five years old. How could you have known, and even if you had, there would have been nothing that you could have done. None of this was your fault. But let's stop for tonight. We both need some rest. Tomorrow we will talk some more."

"I could stay up all night to hear the rest of the story, but you are right, Sis. We do need to get some sleep. It is pretty late, and it has been a very long day." And with that brother and sister hugged each other one last time before they went up to their rooms.

※

Zack and Maya slept until almost noon the next day.

"I can't remember ever sleeping that late," Zack told his sister.

"That makes two of us," Maya replied. "But let's go get some breakfast, or should I say lunch? And then we will go into town and see what trouble we can get into." They both laughed as they walked toward the kitchen.

That afternoon, they bought some odds and ends and finally made their way back to the house.

"I cannot wait," Zack told his sister, "until we can sit outside and you can tell me the rest of what happened to you and Bryan." And so it was. After dinner, they cleaned their dishes, took a bottle of wine, and made themselves comfortable on Maya's patio.

After ten minutes of silence, each of them deep into their own thoughts, Maya began to continue her story.

"I woke up the next morning feeling very confused. Where was I? And then it all came back to me. I no longer was at Weekend Retreat. I was in a shelter. I got dressed, went downstairs, and found Pam in the kitchen having breakfast.

"'There you are. Just in time to join me. She gave me a huge smile. I was hungry, and after we ate, I began to talk. I told her what I had done at the retreat, and I told her about Bryan and you. Pam listened intently to every word.

"'Hmm,' she said. 'You seem to be very smart even though you did not have a chance to finish school, and you also worked in nursing. First, you need to finish school, and if you can do that, I will help you to get into nursing school so you can become a registered nurse, and that way you will never have to worry about having a job.'

"'You can do all this?' I could not believe what she was telling me.

"'Yes, I can,' she answered. 'There are government programs I have access to, but you will have to study hard.'

"'Oh, I will,' I told her. I really wanted to hug her, but I was too shy to do so.

"',' in the meantime she continued, 'I will try to find out what happened to your two brothers and see if I can locate them.'

"And so it was. I studied hard and graduated. And after that I started nursing school. Pam had also arranged for me to have room and board at the community hospital in exchange for twenty hours of work per week. So, little brother, you can see I had no time for anything other than schoolwork, eating, and sleeping, but I was happy, really happy. I visited Pam as often as I could, and then the day came when she told me that she had located you. I remember searching her face, but she shook her head. She had read my mind. 'Not yet, but we are not giving up. There is no trace of Bryan. I don't understand this myself, but I promise you I will keep searching. Sooner or later, we will find something.'

And So Time Went By

Now I had only six months left until I would graduate and be a registered nurse when I got very sick one afternoon. Lucky for me, I was at the hospital when it happened, so the doctors were able to take tests right away to see what was going on. Half an hour later, they told me, 'You have a ruptured appendix. We need to operate right away.' Looking at my face, they joked. 'Don't worry; you don't need that thing anyway.'

"I was confused. 'No, no, that cannot be.' I told them my appendix ruptured when I was still living at Weekend Retreat and that was almost four years ago. I remember the doctors looking at each other in total confusion. Then they told me, 'Let's go and get an MRI so we can see exactly what is going on here.' And so we did.

An hour later, I found myself in the chief of staff's office with the two doctors who had examined me.

"'Maya, sit down,' the chief of staff told me gently. I need to ask you some questions.'

I remember being very scared. 'Am I going to die?' I finally asked.

"'Oh, nothing like that, the three doctors answered at the same time. 'But you need to go way back into your memory, and you need to tell us everything—and I mean everything—about your stay at Weekend Retreat.'

I must have looked very scared, but I was reassured that nothing that I would tell them would ever leave the office. So I started talking, and I told them about everything that had happened at Weekend Retreat. When I was finished, they informed me that I still had my appendix, which they would have to take out now, but that I was short one kidney. What the doctors had taken at the retreat was one of my kidneys.

"There's a lot of money to be made in the black market for organs," was the next thing that they told me.

"'Are you sure?' I could not believe what I was hearing. 'Are you one hundred percent sure?'

"'Yes, we are,' was their answer. 'We have heard rumors that there was more going on at the retreat than babysitting, but those were only rumors. Nobody could ever prove anything. But let's take care of you first. We will talk about this more when you are well.'

"And so it was. In no time, they had me prepped for surgery, and the last thing that I remember was the chief of staff holding my hand, smiling gently, and whispering, 'You are going to be fine. I am doing this operation myself.'

"A few hours later, when I started to wake up in the recovery room, the first thing that I saw was all three doctors sitting in chairs around my bed watching me. 'Don't you have anything to do?' I heard myself saying. They all stood up at once to lean over me.

"'Hello, beautiful. How are you feeling?'

"'Hungry and thirsty,' I told them.

"'Oh, that's good.' They laughed a happy laugh. Zack let me tell you I felt so loved at that moment, and for the first time in such a long time, I felt safe. It was like I had found a new family. The only thing that was missing was you and Bryan my two brothers. I recovered very quickly and was ready to go back to work when the chief of staff invited me to his house for a small dinner party.

"'Come and meet my wife.' He told me. 'And by the way, my name is Christopher. You can call me that away from the hospital.'

"'Oh, I cannot do that,' I told him. 'But I will call you. Dr. C.'

"He laughed. 'Well, tomorrow night then. Seven o'clock.' And then he handed me a piece of paper with his address.

"The next day, I started to feel a little uneasy. What should I wear? Was this a formal dinner? I remembered some of the dinner parties at our parents' house when they were still alive. The women wore long evening gowns, something that I did not even own, but then I told myself, 'Relax, Maya. Had it been formal, Dr. C would have told me.' The only nice garment that I owned was a beautiful black silk pantsuit I had splurged on in a weak moment. I would wear that. It would be all right whether or not the party was formal. That thought put me in a relaxed mood, and I really started looking forward to the evening.

The Next Night

I remember sitting in my beat-up little car for a few minutes, just staring at the house. It was so beautiful, like our parents' house. I had almost forgotten that people really lived like this. Finally, I got out of my car, took the little bouquet of flowers that I had bought to give to Dr. C's wife, and walked slowly up to the front door. It opened before I could ring the bell.

"'There you are.' Dr. C hugged me gently; then he turned to the lady beside him. 'This is our little Maya.' And to me, he said, 'This is my wife, Francesca.' We looked at each other and instantly felt like we had known each other forever.

"I handed Francesca her bouquet of fresh flowers. It seemed so small among all the beautiful large bouquets throughout the house. But then I saw the joy in her eyes. 'I have not had flowers this beautiful in years,' she whispered to me. 'But now let's go to the dining room so I can introduce you to the rest of the guests.'

"The evening was fun. Francesca stayed by my side like a mother protecting her child. When I was ready to leave, she told me to stay a little while longer. 'My husband and I would like to talk to you.' Confused, I stayed. And after the last of the guests had gone, we sat down in the living room. Dr. C got us a brandy, and I waited nervously to hear what they wanted to talk to me about. Finally, he told me, 'Maya, you are still living in that tiny room at the hospital. We would like for you to live here with us. We have a beautiful little guesthouse. You will have your own space. I told my wife your history, but I wanted her to meet you first before we made you the offer to stay with us.'"

I could not believe what I was hearing. Tears came into my eyes, but Francesca took my hand and said, 'Please, Maya, do come and live with us. I could tell from the moment I saw you that we would become the best of friends. I never had a daughter, just sons, and you feel like a daughter to me already.'

"'I don't know if I can afford the rent on your guesthouse,' I told them. 'I don't make much money yet as a nurse." Francesca looked confused, but Dr. C laughed out loud. "You don't pay us any rent; you don't pay for anything. We want you to live here, period.'

"'Oh, but—'

"'No buts.' He went on. 'Tomorrow we will move you; it's all settled.'

"And that, my little brother is how I came to live with Dr. C and Francesca until I bought this house.

※

Like the two evenings before, Zack and Maya took their bottle of wine and settled back into their chairs on the patio, and after a few minutes, Maya continued her story.

"Life was beautiful. I had my own space; the Cs. never invaded my privacy, but yet we were together almost every evening. They had become the parents I never had. The only thing in my life that was missing was you and Bryan. I had located you, but there was no trace of Bryan. It was like he had never existed. One night, Dr. C told me that he wanted to talk to me about something very, very serious. He said, 'Tonight if possible.' I nodded my head and told him, 'Tonight is fine.' When I got to the house, I saw that Dean and Paul, the other two doctors, were also there. I did not know what to think. Did I do something wrong at the hospital? I started to get very nervous. Maybe they wanted me to move. After all, I had already lived with them for over two years

"'Do you want me to move?' I finally asked.

For a moment, Dr. C was startled, but then he laughed. 'Move?' he said. 'No, we don't want you to move. You can stay here for the rest of your life if you want to. No, this is about something totally different. It concerns your brother Bryan.'

"'You found him? Is he all right?'

"'No,' Dr. C. answered. 'This is just the thing that we cannot figure out. There is no trace of him. It is like he never existed. But I have a plan, and that is what I want to talk to you about.'

He hesitated for a moment but then continued

"'Maya, you are a registered nurse with excellent credentials now. For you to ever find out what happened to your brother, you need to go back to Weekend Retreat.'

"I turned white. I felt sick. 'I can't,' I told him. 'Just to think of that place makes me want to throw up.'

"'Maya, hear me out,' Dr. C went on. 'We have a plan. You need to get a job there. We will have to change your name and your appearance. I will take care of all the paper work and Francesca will take care of the rest. Also, you will not be the only one going in there. Dean and Paul will also try to get jobs there.' Again, he told me, 'You will not totally be alone.'

"'But now, to another matter. Did you not tell us that Zack, your baby brother, is a private detective? We would also like to recruit him to help because it looks like this will be the only chance that we will ever have to find out what happened to Bryan and also uncover what is really going on at the retreat Dean, Paul, and I have been talking about this plan for almost a year now. We just needed to make sure that you were mentally ready and that we could get Zack on board to help. It will be very dangerous. These are dangerous and greedy people who control that organization, but this is the only way, because if we are right, there is a lot more going on in there than any of us even realize. But enough talk for tonight. Sleep on it, Maya. We will talk about this more over the next few weeks. Zack I am telling you, I could not believe what they were asking me, going back to that place was out of the question I shook my head and said, "I am not going back to the retreat I am never going back to that hell hole that brought me nothing but pain. And then I asked myself, "why was I so stupid to ever mention that you had become a private detective?"

※

But we did talk. We planned this down to the smallest little detail. I bought my house in my new name so there would be no connection with my old life, and this is why I pleaded with you to leave your busy schedule and come and visit me. We need you to be on board with us.

"Now that I told you the whole story, will you consider helping us? You will also have to change your name, and I don't know what job you would apply for, but really the only important thing is that we get inside and that we become trustworthy to them."

Maya looked into Zack's eyes. She could not tell what he was thinking. His face was like a mask. She started to worry. He was only twenty-two years old. Maybe this was too much for him to handle. But then she felt his hand on her cheek and heard his voice telling her, "Count me in, Maya. I will be with you one hundred percent. We will find out what happened to our brother and your kidney and whatever else that is going on in there." They both cried now, but they were happy tears. They talked a little while longer but finally made their way to their rooms. Tomorrow, Zack would meet Dr. C and the two other doctors.

※

Two months later they were in. They had gotten the jobs. Maya, Dean, and Paul were making last minute preparations. We don't like our staff to leave the premises too often we have everything that you would ever need right here. Each of them had been told the same thing when they received the call that they had been hired. So this meeting tonight was a little bit of a goodbye for all of them—for how long, nobody really knew.

"If I remember correctly, we may not see each other for a while," Maya told them. "There are so many buildings on the premises. I never saw Bryan in all those years. But since we are staff members, hopefully we will have a little more freedom.

"Zack has the best job to find out what is going on since he moves the guests from building to building. He's already been working for almost three weeks now. Just everybody be careful." Dr. C's voice sounded a little shaky. "And try to watch out for each other."

"We will," Maya, Dean, and Paul promised him as they stood up to leave.

"I will pray for your safety every single day." Francesca had tears in her eyes as she hugged Maya one last time.

Dean, Paul, and Maya went home. She would start working tomorrow, Dean and Paul the following week.

Bryan, if you are still there, I promise I will find you, were her last thoughts; then she closed her eyes to get a few hours of sleep.

Next day

"There you are, Miss Marion. Welcome to Weekend Retreat."

Maya's legs felt like rubber. She looked around; nothing had changed. It felt like time had stood still. She smiled nervously as the doctor shook her hand. She listened to him telling her how impressed he had been with her résumé.

"We are so happy that you have decided to join us, but for now, let me take you to your apartment so you can settle in. Later, you will meet the rest of the staff. We have several new members, so we decided to have a little cocktail party where everybody could meet at the same time. But here we are." He started to open a door. "Welcome to your new life. Someone will pick you up at six o'clock." And with that, he left.

Maya stood inside her new home. It was beautiful and surprisingly large, nothing like the small, dingy room that she had lived in for so many years. This place never ceased to amaze her.

"I need to freshen up and get ready for tonight," she told herself. She took a quick shower and then decided on a simple black dress. Would there be anybody that could recognize her? She could not stop her heart from pounding. "Relax," she reminded herself. Francesca had worked a miracle. Her eyes were no longer blue, thanks to colored contact lenses, and her hair was no longer blonde; it was a rich, chestnut brown. "I don't even recognize myself," and with that conclusion, she started feeling better. *Bryan, I am here to find you* were her last thoughts when she heard a knock on the door.

The little party was in full swing when Maya stepped in to the ballroom. She looked around to see a familiar face but did not recognize anybody. *Where was Zack?* She wondered? But then she saw Dean and Paul. They were introduced. "Have you seen Zack?" Maya asked her two friends the first chance she had. "No," they told her, "but don't worry. We are the elite group here, and Zack is considered beneath us. After all, he just transports people from building to building." That made sense to her. Still in her own thoughts, she felt a hand on her shoulder.

"Ms. Marion, meet our founder and the most important man of Weekend Retreat. When she turned, she looked into that same cruel face that she so well remembered from years ago. But now that face was smiling sweetly. As he shook her hand, he told her how pleased he was that she had decided to join his staff. "We only hire the very best." *Yes, I bet you do,* Maya thought, *to remove organs and what-*

ever else it is that you do you need the very best. But she smiled and reassured him how pleased she was to be there. Then he introduced her to some of the doctors that she would be working with, and luckily one of them was Paul.

The alarm woke her up the next morning. She took a quick shower, put on her uniform, and went to have breakfast. Then she followed a nurse to her new workstation. What she saw made her blood run cold. There were the cots with the sleeping children. Everything came back to her like it was yesterday, only this time she was the one who administered the shots to wake the children up. She did not have to ask questions; after all, she knew the routine. She saw the other nurse looking at her a couple of times, but she went on with her duties like it was the most natural thing to do.

That went on for about three weeks when one day she was called to the chief's office. Not knowing what to expect, she felt cold chills running down her spine, but the man smiled and told her, "Ms. Marion, I have heard nothing but the very best about your performance, so we have decided to promote you to a different facility. People like you who don't ask questions will have a brilliant future with us.

"You will be assisting in some very delicate surgeries. This is not only a retreat but also a very special hospital. People get sick even on vacation, and since we are the finest retreat in the country, naturally we are equipped to take care of sick people too." And, before she could ask anything else she was excused. Her mind was racing. *Bryan, I am getting closer to find out what happened to you all these years ago,* she thought as she went back to work.

The next day, she started her new job.

"We only have two surgeries today," she was told by one of the doctors when two orderlies brought the first stretcher in. Maya looked at a young boy; he could not have been more than sixteen years old. She saw fear in his eyes, but she took his hand, and with her soft voice, she reassured him that he was in good hands and that he would be all right. Then she watched in horror as the doctors removed one of his kidneys, laughing and joking the whole time. Later, she did not remember how she had gotten through the surgery, but for now she was sitting in the recovery room holding the young man's hand.

Finally, he woke up and tried to smile. "Is it over?" she heard him whisper. "Did they take my bad appendix out?"

"It is over," Maya reassured him. "You are going to be just fine."

"Thank you," she heard him say as she

watched him to go back to sleep. This went on at least twice a week.

One day, a van pulled up with four young men and two young girls. They could not have been more than seventeen years old. Soon she found out that they came from an orphanage. They had never been adopted and Maya could tell that they were very grateful to come to Weekend Retreat.

They were put into her care. She had to make sure that they were healthy and that their organs were strong. Maya knew what was going to happen to them, but there was nothing that she could do. She got really attached to one of the girls, and she knew the young woman felt about her the same way. Two of the boys had already made it through their surgery when the unthinkable happened. The third boy was on the operating table when Maya realized that the doctors were removing the second kidney. She froze and stammered, "You cannot do this; he won't live."

"No, he won't," was the cold answer from one of the doctors. "But someone with his rare blood type and a lot of money will." And with that, he continued the surgery. Then she watched in horror as two orderlies wrapped the body in a plastic bag and wheeled him out of the room. One of the doctors turned to her and whispered, "It happens all the time. Nobody will miss him. Remember, he was an orphan."

Like Bryan and me, she thought. *Is that what happened to Bryan? Oh dear God.* "Where will they take the body?" she whispered. She was told that there was a crematorium on the premises and the he would be cremated.

That evening, Maya could not eat or sleep. The pieces started to come together. *I guess I am lucky to be alive she thought, they only took one of my kidneys.*

Over the next few months, several young boys lost their lives. Maya had seen Dean and Paul only once and Zack not at all. She really started to get worried about Zack. Where was he? Weekend Retreat was large but not so large that they would not cross paths at least once. She had applied for a weekend pass, weeks ago and finally she was told that she could take three days. She would see Dr. C and Francesca; maybe they had heard from Zack.

The day finally came, and now she was standing at Dr. C's front door. Before she could ring the bell, the door flew open. They did not know she was coming; she had been afraid to contact them. Weekend Retreat monitored everybody so close, and after all, she was there under a false identity. Dr. C hugged her, and Francesca cried; they were both so happy to see her.

"We were beginning to really get worried," they told her. "We have seen Zack, Dean, and Paul. Zack is fine." Maya was relieved. "They are all fine; we mostly worried about you." Then they started talking. Maya told them what she knew, and they told her what the others had found out.

The Retreat did not only deal in organs but also had a huge market for babies. There was another building on the premises where they inseminated young, healthy girls that mostly came from orphanages to sell their babies on the black market to rich couples. That's where Dean was working. Zack had actually transported these girls many times. However, some of the women who would not get pregnant were then sent over where Maya worked to donate one or two organs.

Now even more things were falling into place. She had always wondered why there were so many more boys than girls used for these surgeries. Now she knew the girls were used to have babies.

Could this get any worse? And how would they ever prove any of this? They all looked at each other, but nobody had an answer.

※

The three days went by much too fast, and Maya was now back at Weekend Retreat. The holidays were getting close, and the retreat was busy planning some very fancy parties. Businessmen from all over the country attended most of them with girls on their arms who were younger than their daughters.

Maya, who now belonged to the upper staff, was invited to all of them. She sometimes really did not want to attend, but declining was not an option.

At one of the parties, she noticed a doctor watching her very carefully. At first she felt uneasy. Did he recognize her from somewhere? But when he finally approached her and started talking, she felt no fear. It seemed like she knew him even though they had never met.

"My name is Trevor," he told her. "And you are?" She told him Marion, and after that they just talked. She found out that he had started working at the retreat two months ago but that he was short one nurse.

"Would you like to start working with me? I could put in a request. "He looked at her Maya did not know what to say, but he just smiled and told her, "I will take care of everything; just leave it to me."

He had meant every word and three weeks later, she was again in a totally different section of the retreat, working with Trevor.

"How big is this place?" she asked him one day.

"Something like three hundred acres," he told her. "We are a city. I have been here three months now, and I still don't know everything that's on these premises."

Maya thought, *I lived here half of my life, and I know less than you*, but she kept that thought to herself.

So in this building was also the incubator. There were over one hundred and fifty girls there, either pregnant or waiting to get pregnant. Maya often felt like crying when she looked into the hopeless faces of these girls. Then one day something happened that changed everything. A beautiful seventeen-year-old girl just would not get pregnant. They had tried to inseminate her several times, but it just did not happen. Maya knew what came next. The girl would be sent over to Trevor for organ donation. She walked over to the bed and nearly cried out. It was the same girl that she had gotten so attached to a few months back. What had they done to her? She was just a shadow of herself.

"What will they do to me now?" Maya barely heard the question.

"You will go over to another building away from all these pregnant women." She tried to sound cheerful. "I work over there, so I will see you tomorrow."

Back in the other section, Maya felt Trevor looking at her intensely. "What happened?" he finally asked. "Please talk to me. I promise it will be safe."

Maya told him about the girl. "They're sending two over tomorrow, and she is one of them. I am not sure I can assist you in that surgery."

That night, after everybody had retired, Maya heard a knock on her door. It was Trevor.

"Follow me," he told her. "And don't say a word." She did as she was told and watched as Trevor went straight to the girl's bed, gave her an injection, and wrapped her into a bag that was used for the dead. Her own body felt paralyzed but then she saw her little brother, Zack. Not one word was spoken. Both men put the body on the stretcher, and seconds later, Zack and the girl were out the door.

"What is going on? What just happened here?" She looked at Trevor. He did not speak; he just gave her a look that told her that the girl would be all right. Totally confused, she heard his voice now telling her to follow him to his office. Once there, he said, "Sit down, Maya. It is time for us to talk." Still in shock, she listened as he told her that Dr. C and Francesca were his parents. "I am also here under cover, just like the rest of you. Zack knows who I am. He is the only one. We have been working together for several months now. We are trying to save as many lives as we can. We cannot save them all, but the girl that he just picked up is going to be fine. My dad and some others are helping from the outside. We have established a safe house. I am keeping records. Trust me, Maya. We are getting closer, and the day will come when we will shut this place down.

"Bryan?" Maya asked, "Have you found out anything about my brother?"

"Not yet," Trevor told her, "but we keep searching. Believe me when I tell you that we are not giving up. I know that the records of the orphans who have died were destroyed, but records like yours and your brother's are here somewhere. Since your parents had left a lot of money, plus your trust fund, nobody can deny that the three of you existed. I have a strong suspicion of what could have happened to Bryan, but I cannot prove it yet. We had a sixteen-year-old boy about four months ago who was scheduled for one kidney, but these butchers removed both. They thought he was an orphan when in fact he was the son of a very wealthy family who had taken a six-month vacation. It was a real mess. In fact, it still is, especially since the retreat had no authority to have the body cremated."

Maya fully understood what Trevor was telling her. She shook. "Do you think that that's what happened to Bryan?"

"That is the only possible answer that we can come up with for now. There are no records of any kind, and since your parents had died, they did not think that they would ever have to answer to anybody later."

"How can they get away with all this and for so many years? Why hasn't anybody ever asked questions?"

"The world is corrupt, Maya. Money is power. You can buy yourself almost out of any crime, and parents are so involved with their own lives; they really don't know anything about their children."

Maya could not argue with that; her parents, especially her mother, never had heard a thing her children tried to tell her. But then Trevor went on. "We are getting closer; we have to be even more careful, but we are getting closer." With that, they said good night, and Maya left to go to her own quarters.

During the days, Maya and Trevor hardly spoke to each other. They did not really need to. One look and they knew what the other one was thinking. But often during late-night hours, they talked and tried to figure out how to get to the files.

One evening, Trevor told Maya, "Nobody has heard from Paul for several months now, not even my father. He is getting very worried that something has happened to him. Dean and Zack don't know anything either. But there is supposed to be a cocktail party coming up soon. Maybe we will see Paul there."

Three weeks later, invitations to the party arrived. It was to be the most exquisite event the retreat had ever seen, and they had seen some fancy ones. This one was black tie only. Maya had bought a beautiful, long, black gown. She still got chills when she thought about the price tag, but so what? She certainly could afford it. The retreat paid their doctors and surgical nurses very well.

One last look into the mirror and then she stepped outside and onto the cart that would take her to the building were the party took place.

What a beautiful sight, she thought. The music, the lights—it looked like a fairy tale. The retreat really had gone all out on this event. It had to be very special. *Just try to have a good time,* she told herself when dark thoughts were trying to take over. *This is just one evening, and maybe we will see Paul and get some news.*

Then she felt a hand on her arm.

"You look absolutely beautiful." She heard Trevor's low voice. Why was her heart pounding? She felt like … oh, she did not know what she felt. It was something new and wonderful. She smiled happily, took his arm, and together they walked into the ballroom. They had some champagne, danced, and mingled. They found Dean and talked to him.

"Have you seen Paul?" Trevor asked.

"Not for about seven weeks now," Dean told them. "I saw him getting out of a car once, but I did not get to talk to him. I am also getting worried. He should be here tonight, but if he is not, well, we don't even want to think about that." But before they could talk any further, they heard a bell ring and a voice telling them to get ready for a very special announcement.

The room got so quiet you could have heard a needle drop. Then a huge door opened, and Paul walked through it with a beautiful woman on his arm. Then they heard the voice from the man who owned Weekend Retreat.

"Welcome, everybody, welcome. It gives me the greatest pleasure to announce the engagement of my only child, my beautiful daughter, Rebecca, to Paul Bremer, one of our most promising doctors."

Maya started to feel sick. She felt Trevor's Arm tightening around her waist holding her up. Could this be happening? If this was real, they were all in great danger.

"Maybe there is an explanation for this," she whispered to Trevor. But they all could tell by Paul's face that this was not a show. He had gone over to the other side. Maya, Dean, and Zack were indeed in great danger. Their lives hung in mid air. Thank God Paul did not know about Trevor. Dr. C had thought it best to keep that hidden. And for that Maya thanked him silently.

By now everybody stood in line to congratulate the newly engaged couple. "Smile and look happy" was the last thing Maya heard Trevor whisper, and then she stood in front of Paul. He smiled a sarcastic smile as she congratulated him.

"So you are Nurse Marion," How nice to finally meet you. I have heard some very good things about you." Was that the same man she thought she knew? She felt a shiver. His smile had changed as he went on talking. "My fiancée and I are going away for a few days, but after we return, I will have a private visit with each of my staff members, and that includes you." His eyes looked dangerous and cold now. He was warning her, and she knew it. Until later then he said and Maya knew she was dismissed. She grabbed the first glass of champagne she saw and drank it as fast as she could. Then she turned to look back at the happy couple.

After that, Maya could not wait for the party to end. She had felt Paul's cold eyes watching her several times, but she had also learned to play the game. After all, she was here at the retreat, a place that she hated more than anything in her life. *So you want to play, you bastard,* she thought. *Well then, let's play.*

After the party they did not see Dean for several weeks.

"Do you think that he left the retreat?" Maya asked Trevor one day at work, but before he could answer, the doors opened and two more bodies were wheeled in for kidney donation.

"They're already prepped," the orderlies told them. Maya looked at their faces and nearly cried out. One of them was Dean. Trevor walked over to look and then said with a calm voice, "Well then, let's get started." Then he turned to Maya and said in a low voice, "Don't make a scene right now. Don't ask questions. You need to trust me and do exactly as I tell you."

She watched as Trevor removed one kidney from the first patient. Then he filled out Dean's chart and called a nurse to take him to recovery. Then she watched in horror as he removed the second kidney and filled out the paperwork. Then the boy was moved to the recovery room where Maya knew he would not recover.

She felt Trevor looking at her. His eyes told her that this had been the only way to save Dean. She understood and prayed to God to forgive them. Later that evening, she watched as her brother wheeled Dean out of their ward, hopefully to safety.

※

The following week, she was called into Paul's office.

"Sit down," he told her. "I am only going to say this once. I have a proposition for you. I know why we came here." He continued "But you must realize how many lives we are saving with our organs. Life presents choices, and I have chosen but this is not about me this is about you. Now you will have to choose. You are an excellent nurse, and we would like for you to consider spending the rest of your life here as part of our family. You will have everything your heart desires and more. Think about it very, very carefully. I expect an answer from you within a week. In the meantime, you are not allowed to leave these premises. I do hope you understand. This is in everybody's best interest, especially yours." And with those words, she was dismissed. Maya understood. Oh, yes, she understood only too well. It had been a warning. He might as well have told her, "You either are with us or against us, and if you are not with us, you will never leave these premises alive." Oh, yes, she fully understood.

She needed to talk to Trevor as soon as possible. They were all in danger of losing their lives.

Later that evening, she told Trevor almost word for word off her conversation that morning with Paul.

"The time has come for us to make our move Trevor said quietly you are right; this has become a life-threatening situation. Tell Paul that after careful consideration, you have decided to stay at the retreat. Tell him whatever is necessary. And what you think that he needs to hear I have to know that you are safe. In the meantime, I will get all of my papers together and contact my dad on the outside. It should only take a few more days, but until the last details are in place, you need to play your part."

And Maya did. On her next meeting with Paul, she told him that she would be happy to stay. When he looked at her with great suspicion, she reassured him, "Paul, I have no family, and I am a good nurse, so why would I not want to stay here? After all, the retreat is doing good work, and also,

I could never make the money that I am making here in another hospital. I would be foolish to leave."

He seemed convinced, he studied her and finally, he spoke. "I am so glad that you came to your senses. After all the past is the past, and it should be forgotten." She smiled to his face, but in her heart she felt nothing bur raw hate for this man. How could someone she thought she knew change so much in such a short time? Money! Trevor was right when he had told her that some people would do anything for money. "Well, then Paul smiled congratulations on your decision." And with that, Maya was dismissed.

She could not help but smile to herself. Indeed she had become a very good actress.

Another week went by when Trevor told Maya everything was in place. "All the files are in my father's possession, and in a few days, things will start to crash down hell will break loose, so be prepared." But that was not to be.

"Where is Nurse Marion? I cannot do these surgeries by myself." Trevor was running around like a madman. "Did you find her?" he yelled at the nurse.

"No, I don't know where she is. I checked her apartment. All her clothes are gone, but nobody seems to know anything more."

Oh dear God Trevor could not breathe. Then another orderly came through the door and told him, "Miss Marion had to leave. For how long, nobody knows. Her mother had gotten very ill, and she needed to care for her. But another nurse will arrive shortly to assist you with your surgeries."

I need to talk to Paul. Trevor tried to stay calm. The sooner the better, but before he could make an appointment the new nurse arrived so they could go on with their scheduled surgeries. That afternoon, he dialed the number to Paul's office and requested to talk to him. They had only met a few times at parties and that was in his favor. He also had no doubt that Maya was somewhere on the premises because he knew that her parents had been killed years ago when they were children. In fact, he knew their whole history from his mom and dad. So everything that the orderly had told him this morning had been a lie. The only thing that he did not know was why. What could have possibly gone wrong? He wondered about Zack and hoped that he was safe. And what about him? Did they know who he really was? *Well, I will have to take a chance and find out, so the sooner, the better.*

"I am sorry," the secretary told Trevor, "but Paul left his office early. He will be at his future father-in-law's house at a cocktail party and has given strict orders not to be disturbed. Also, he will not be in all day tomorrow. You can have an appointment the day after that. Shall we say after lunch?" Trevor was furious but realized that he had no choice but to tell the woman that he gladly accepted that time.

"Well, then we shall see you day after tomorrow," she said once more, and with that the conversation was over. Trevor stared at the phone for a long time day after tomorrow. It seemed like an eternity.

"Maya, where are you? Are you even alive? I cannot think like that," he told himself. "She has to be alive." He suddenly realized that she meant much more to him than just a friend. "I am in love with her." It hit him hard. "I cannot lose her. I will not lose her, and with that, he found new strength. Maya, I will find you," he whispered. "Wherever you are, I will find you."

※

The next day passed slowly, but finally he stood in Paul's office.

"I remember you." Paul shook his hand. He was smiling. "You are one of our best doctors. Sit down. What can I do for you?"

Play the part, Trevor told himself. *Maya's life depends on it.*

"I have a situation," Trevor started. "As you know, I have these delicate Surgeries every day, and my nurse, Marion, is on leave. I have had two different nurses since, but both of them have made mistakes so that the organs could not be used. It takes a very skillful nurse to handle this, and I have never worked with a better nurse than Ms. Marion. Now, my question to you is can we hold off on these surgeries until she returns, because losing these organs is costing us a lot of money, and that is, after all, not what we are here for, to lose money, right?" Trevor looked directly at Paul, who had not said a word. Finally, he smiled.

"I like you, Trevor. I like the way you think. I will have to promote you. You are definitely an asset to our organization but now about your nurse. Let me see if I can find out how her mother is coming along. Hopefully you will have her back soon." Then he added, "I am glad that you came to me so quickly with your problem. We cannot afford to lose more organs. Go ahead and cancel your surgeries for the next four days, and I will let you know what I find out about Nurse Marion's mother." And with that, Trevor was excused.

On his way back to his building, his mind wandered to Maya. *Hold on, my darling. I'm doing my best to rescue you. I hope that lying bastard believes what I told him that I cannot do surgeries successfully without my nurse. Hopefully his greed will set you free. He also said something about four days. Did they put you to sleep? Something made him do this, but what? I have so many questions and no answers. If they put you to sleep, that means you are alive for the time being.*

Then Trevor told himself, "I need to get a message to my father right away not to make a move from the outside until I know you are safe. Now back at his station, he canceled all of his surgeries. The orderly and his new nurse looked at him in confusion.

"Doctor, the patient is prepped and ready to go."

"So what?" he yelled at her. "Take him back to his room and let him sleep it off. You also don't need to come back. I'd like to be alone for the rest of the day." She looked at him confused but then wheeled her patient out as quickly as she could.

What an ass, she thought. *I am not sure I can work with him.*

Trevor went to his office, and his secret hiding place where he kept his little pager. Then he sent an urgent message to his father to stop the invasion until further notice. He knew that his father would panic, but he could not go into details right now. He really was not even sure that sending messages from his pager was safe. Then he got last-minute details together; things could happen now very fast.

"If I could, I would leave tonight," he told himself. "But I cannot leave Maya behind. Also, where is Zack? I have not seen him. I need to get a hold of him. Maybe he will know something." And with that, he went to his phone to contact him. A strange voice answered. "Where is your other transporter?" Trevor asked the man. "I don't know was the answer. He was lying on a cot when I got here. They told me he was sick," Trevor slammed the phone down and ran as fast as he could to the room where the future donors were kept. He went from bed to bed; then his heart stopped. The patient who had been prepped for surgery right after he had talked to Paul was Zack. *Oh, dear God,* he thought. *Now I know for sure that something has gone very wrong. Paul was trying to kill Zack and Maya.* He gave Zack a shot. "Wake up," he prayed. "You need to wake up if you want to live." His prayer was answered. Zack started to move his hands. Trevor gave him another shot;

then he watched him open his eyes. He could tell that Zack recognized him. He pulled him into a sitting position.

"Listen to me very careful he told him I need to hide you for a few hours in my apartment. By then, your head should be clear. You need to get off these premises while it is still dark outside and get in contact with my father. We now cannot wait any longer. Can you do this?"

Zack nodded his head. "I know how to leave this place without being seen. I know these grounds like the back of my hand."

"Good. Then let's get you out of here to a safe place."

After Trevor had Zack in his room, he went back to find a place for the cot. Nothing could look suspicious, and after that was done, he felt a little easier. Now if he could only locate Maya.

Evening finally came, and when things got quiet, Trevor helped Zack slip out of the building. "Be safe," he prayed as he watched his friend disappear into the night.

He was not ready to go back to his apartment, but he also knew that he could not do anything more tonight. So he just sat on the front steps and looked out in to the night. This could have been such a beautiful place, had it not been for all the horrible things that went on inside these walls then he wondered would they be able to shut it down, or would they die trying? That was a big question. Dean was safe on the outside. Now Zack was hopefully out of danger. Just Maya and he were left in here. So far, nobody knew his real identity, or so he hoped, but he also knew if he had Maya with him they would leave this place right now and never look back. And then it became clear. Paul had told him four days. He had his answer. They had put her to sleep. He needed to get to the building where everybody was sleeping. But how was he going to get in there?

※

The next morning, he woke up feeling much better. He knew what he had to do. When his new nurse arrived, he greeted her with a warm smile and a fresh cup of coffee. He could tell that she liked him, and he would use that to his advantage.

"We are not all that busy today," he told her. "Remember, no surgeries."

"I remember." She smiled at him. "But I will be busy. I have two males and a female over at my regular building that needs to be transported next for surgery."

Two males and a female. Trevor's mind was racing, but he quickly caught his breath and told her, "Let's have another cup of coffee, and then if you would like, I can help you bring the next three patients over. She looked at him surprised, but he gave her a big smile and said, "Well, it only makes sense. We have the room right now, and it will save time tomorrow."

She agreed. *He won't be so bad to work with after all,* she thought. *And maybe something more will develop between us. I certainly like him.* And so it was. Trevor also made sure that they ate lunch together. And then they made their way over to the other building. It felt like a morgue, all the sleeping bodies lying on those cots. Trevor felt cold chills running up and down his spine.

"They're not in this room," the nurse told him. "They're in a separate room. I really don't know why, but oh well. It's easier to transport them from there." But here we are, Trevor looked down at the faces, but all he could see was Maya's. That bastard had signed her death warrant. Paul knew that she only had one kidney. He wanted her and Zack to die. "Well, you will not get your wish as long as I'm alive," Trevor murmured.

"Did you say something?" he heard the nurse ask him.

"Yes," he told her. "Let's just take two, and we will get the other one tomorrow. So go ahead. Take the first one, and I will be right behind you with the second one." Works for me she smiled then grabbed the first cot. However as soon as she was out the door, Trevor went quickly to the large room and pulled the first two cots that he could reach into the room were Maya was. Just in case someone would check, there had to be three beds. Then he grabbed Maya's cot and pushed it out of the building.

"What took you so long?" the nurse asked him.

"The cot got stuck between the door, and I had a little trouble getting it loose." His answer satisfied her. She smiled and told him, "It happens sometimes; it has happened to me before." Now they were back at Trevor's building. He needed to take care of Maya; she needed to wake up, but what to do with the nurse?

"Would you like to come over to my place?" he finally asked her. "As I said, we are not busy today. We can talk and get to know each other better."

She did not hesitate. Things were going much better than she had hoped for.

Back in his, apartment Trevor opened a bottle of wine and poured them both a glass.

"To the future, he gave her a big smile.

"To the future," she answered. Little did she know that her future had nothing to do with his?

Trevor watched her closely, and after a few more sips of wine, she went into a deep sleep.

"Sorry about that," he told her. It's nothing personal "I had no choice but to do this." He left quickly to take care of Maya.

Two Hours Later

"Where am I?" Finally, he heard Maya's voice.

"You are here with me and for now you are safe. You need to wake up. Don't ask questions. I will explain everything later. We need to get off these premises as soon as you are strong enough to walk. It has to be tonight. I am afraid by tomorrow it will be too late."

Things slowly started to come back to Maya, and she told Trevor, "The last thing that I remember was Paul giving me a shot and asking me questions. It must have been a truth serum. I don't know what I told him."

You told him plenty, Trevor thought, *enough for him to want to kill you.* But he kept that to himself. "Well, we cannot worry about that right now. We have to get out of here." He went to his private pager and sent his father the signal that said, "Now."

※

It only took a few minutes for the vehicles to arrive. There must have been at least sixty police cars, several fire trucks, and ambulances.

Maya, still very weak, watched as Trevor helped with the sleeping children and the pregnant young girls. Then she saw Paul coming out of the building in handcuffs with the rest of his staff behind him. He looked at her once as he walked by, and she saw more hatred in his eyes than she had ever seen in her entire life. It gave her cold chills, but then he was past her, and she watched the police put him into the van that would take him to jail.

It took several more hours to get all the people out of the different buildings.

"Where are you taking them?" Maya asked one of the officers.

"To a safe place for now, and after that, I really don't know."

After that, it took three more months to clean up the mess inside.

Maya, Trevor, Dean, and Zack helped the prosecution to put everything together to put these butchers behind bars. And after another six months, the day that they all had waited for so long finally arrived.

Everybody was in the courtroom to hear the verdict: guilty, guilty, and guilty on every account.

Tears ran down Maya's cheeks. "Bryan, wherever you are, justice has been done for you and so many others. Now you can rest in peace."

One year later, Maya stood in front of her mirror. She looked good. She felt even better. Trevor was picking her up to take her over to see his parents. They wanted to tell them that they had fallen deeply in love and planned to get married as soon as possible. Francesca cried and hugged Maya over and over. She told her that she had loved her from the first day that they had met. Her fondest wish was coming true. She now had the daughter that she always wanted. Dr. C also tried his best to keep from getting too choked up. *Life was perfect right now,* he thought. He wished that they could hold on to this moment forever. When they heard the doorbell.

"Are you expecting company?" Trevor and Maya both asked at the same time.

"A surprise for both of you," Dr. C said, grinning as he walked toward the front door.

There stood Zack, her little brother, with a beautiful young woman next to him. He smiled. "Meet Elizabeth, my fiancée."

Maya and Trevor stared at the beautiful girl; she looked familiar.

"Have we met?" Maya finally asked. But before she got an answer, Zack told them that she was the girl they had saved that day at the hospital. Maya cried and hugged Elizabeth as Trevor tried to tell his parents the story.

They laughed. "We know everything. After all, Elizabeth has been living in our guesthouse ever since that fateful night."

"Are there any more surprises?" Maya cried.

"Not for tonight," was the answer. "So let's open a bottle of our best. Champagne Tonight, we celebrate." And they did.

Epilogue

Eight years later

The family was at a cocktail party. Trevor and Maya had two sons by now, six and four years old. Zack and Elizabeth had a little girl, three years old. They had named her Angel to thank God for this precious gift. After all, Elizabeth had been scheduled to die at the retreat because they thought that she could not have children. They were in a festive mood; when the unthinkable happened. A couple of their friends invited everybody to join them at their lake house to celebrate the New Year.

"Just us adults they told them so we can really relax and have a good time."

"What about the children?" someone asked.

"Oh, you don't know? We have been taking our children to this wonderful place called Weekend Retreat. It is supposed to be the best in the country."

Trevor looked at his wife. Her face was white as snow.

"What do your children tell you?" he asked the lady. "What did they do for the three or four days while they were there?"

"Well, that's funny," the man said, "they don't tell us anything."

Then his wife chimed in, "My daughter even told me she does not remember. Imagine that. But that's teenagers, I guess. If they don't feel like talking, they just tell you that they don't remember."

Now Trevor felt Maya getting heavy on his arm. He had to get her out of the room quickly before she fainted.

"Excuse us," he told the couple; as they headed to the door.

Who has reopened the retreat? And was the death of Maya, Bryan, and Zack's parents really an accident?